Uh Oh! Gotta Go!

Potty Tales from Toddlers

by Bob McGrath

illustrations by Shelley Dieterichs

BARRON'S

All inquiries should be addressed to:
Barron's Educational Series, Inc.
250 Wireless Boulevard
Hauppauge, New York 11788

ISBN-13: 978-0-8120-6564-0
ISBN-10: 0-8120-6564-6

Library of Congress Catalog Card No. 96-1527

Library of Congress Cataloging-in-Publication Data

McGrath, Bob, 1939-
     Uh oh! gotta go! / by Bob McGrath ; illustrations by
Shelley Dieterichs.
         p.   cm.
     Summary: Twenty-seven vignettes showing a variety of
experiences of many different children during the toilet
training process.
     ISBN 0-8120-6564-6
     1. Toilet training—Juvenile literature. 2. Children—
Health and hygiene—Juvenile literature. [1. Toilet training.]
I. Dieterichs, Shelley, ill. II. Title.
HQ770.5.M4   1996
649'.62—dc20   96-1527
                                                          CIP
Date of Manufacture: September 2016   AC
Manufactured by: M03I03D, Guangdong, China

Printed in China
29 28 27

A Note to the Parents

After five kids and five granddaughters, my wife and I have dealt with a lot of dirty diapers in our lives. We've found that a little sense of humor mixed with potty training goes a long way to relax both parent and child.

Probably no two parents will have the same experience teaching their kids about anything, no matter what the issue. However, if you can trigger a child's sense of imagination and let them discover the humorous side of a situation, whatever it may be, you will have tapped into a very effective problem solving technique.

In the case of our own five kids, and now our five young granddaughters, my wife and I have found that when we use this method it seems to be more effective than taking a more ceremonious approach.

Since there are a number of wonderful potty training books on the market that talk seriously about this subject, we decided to record the potty training process by showing quick episodes that deal with a variety of experiences. Most of these episodes happened to us and our friends.

We hope that your child will find the humor in these vignettes and be able to identify with the kids in them. Since you are your child's first and best teacher, we hope that you will find a lot to talk about in each picture and that they will help to make your child's potty training a fun and successful adventure.

Bob McGrath

Mark picks a potty.

Liam says, "Have potty will travel."

Tammy teaches potty training.

Jermaine announces, "I'm going to the toilet."

Danielle is really proud of her little sister Laura.

Natalie waits and listens for the splash.

Sam is silly.

Sanju raps to "The Potty Beat."

Jordan always waits
for the last minute.

There he goes.

He made it! Hooray!

Toby didn't make it. Toby says, "Not again. I can't believe it." Toby's mom says, "That's okay, Toby."

Alison only uses a grown-up toilet.

Peter stands up like a big man.

Aaron has perfect aim.

Even Queens have to go to the toilet.

Kuniko loves to flush.

Corinne's favorite wipers look like snowballs.
She makes them out of toilet paper.

Amanda goes by the book.

Cathlin plays on the potty.

Look who needs Sonia's diapers now!

Aisha can't wait to wear her underpants.

Derrick empties his bladder
before he rides in the car.

Tom loves everybody's bathroom.

The last thing that Kerry does before
she goes to bed at night is use the potty.

Robert makes the switch at night.

The first time Mario went to the potty,
there was a grand parade.

All my friends love their underpants!

I go to the potty just like all my friends.